Fairy Unicorns

Enchanted River

Zanna Davidson

Illustrated by Nuno Alexandre Vieira

Meet the Unicorns
Zoe
Astra
Sorrel
Unicorn King

Nimbus
Naida
Iris
Shadow

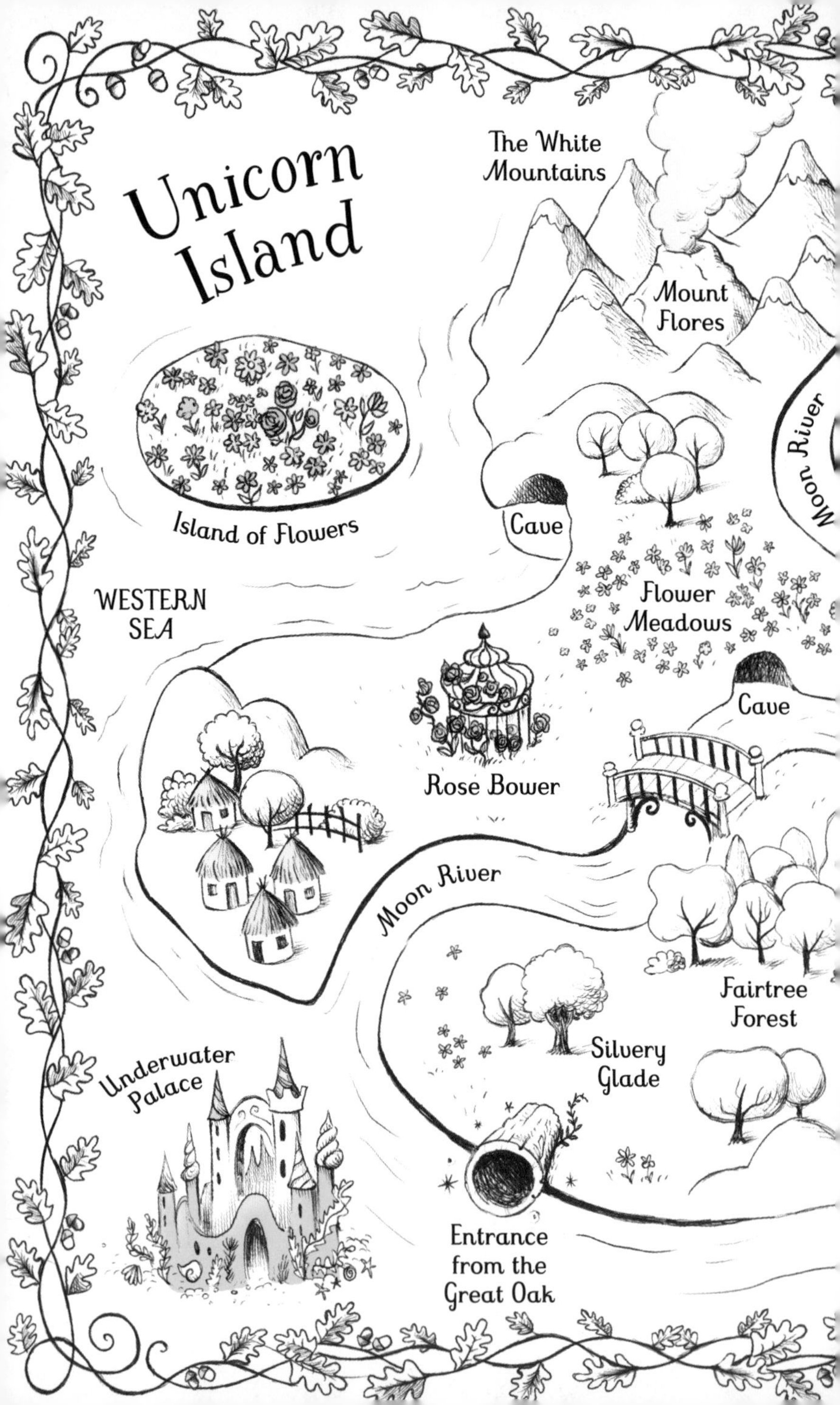
Unicorn Island
The White Mountains
Mount Flores
Moon River
Island of Flowers
Cave
Flower Meadows
WESTERN SEA
Rose Bower
Cave
Moon River
Fairtree Forest
Silvery Glade
Underwater Palace
Entrance from the Great Oak

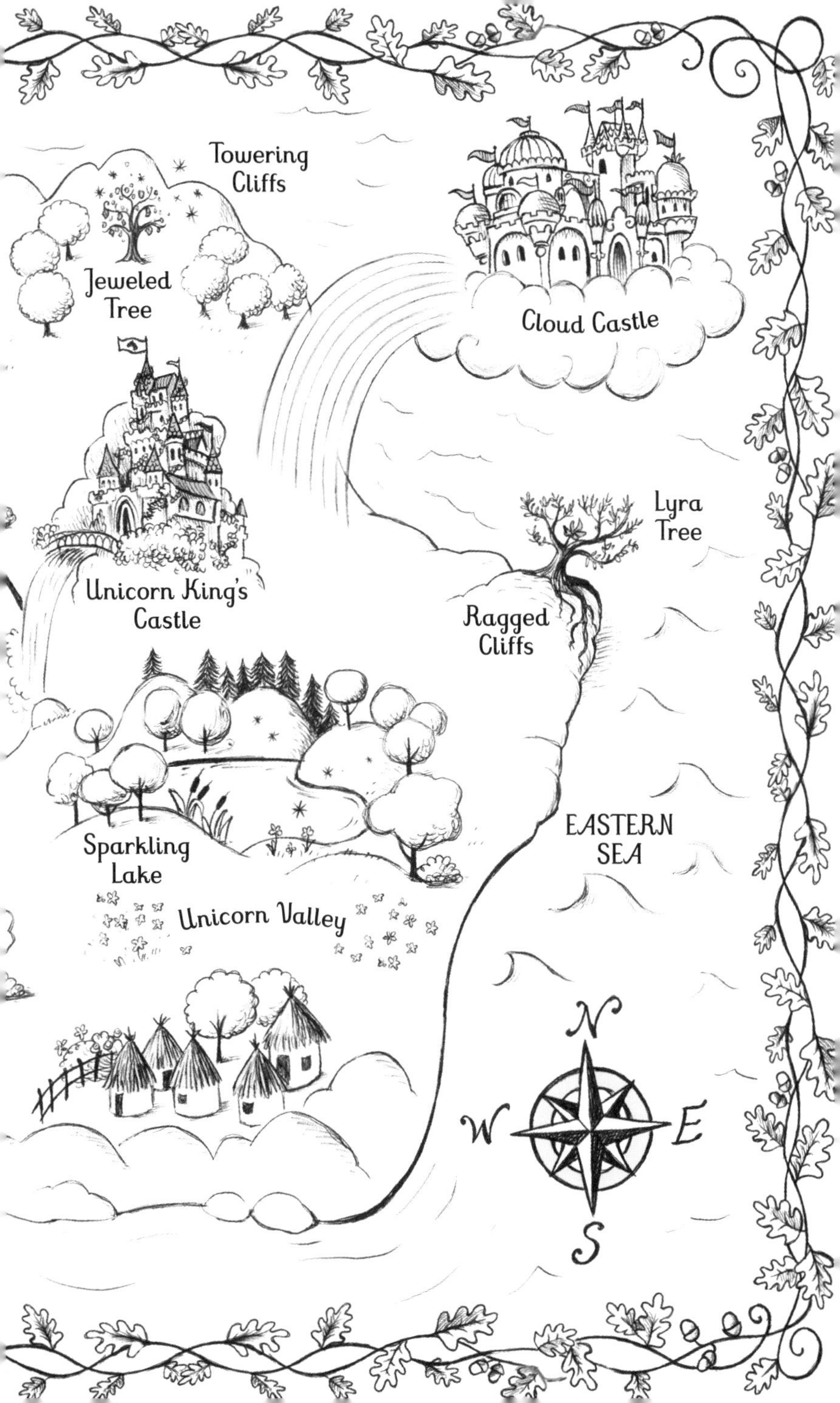
Towering Cliffs
Jeweled Tree
Cloud Castle
Unicorn King's Castle
Lyra Tree
Ragged Cliffs
EASTERN SEA
Sparkling Lake
Unicorn Valley
N
W
E
S

Contents

Chapter One

Zoe waited until the house was quiet and her Great-Aunt May had gone to bed. Then she crept out of her room, down the stairs and through the back door into the garden. The moon shone full and bright in the night sky, showing the way to the oak tree at the end of the path. At the foot of its towering branches, Zoe reached into her pocket and took out a tiny silver bag, which gleamed in the moonlight. She sprinkled herself with its sparkling dust and held her breath…

Yes! There was that familiar, thrilling tingle as the magic began to work. It started in her toes, then spread all over her body, like a sort of fizzing in her veins. Then all of a sudden the world began to look bigger and bigger and Zoe knew she was shrinking. A moment later she was fairy-sized, whispering the words of the spell:

Let me pass into the magic tree,
Where Fairy Unicorns *fly* wild and *free*.
Show me the trail of sparkling light,
To Unicorn Island, shining bright.

A trail of sparkles lit up the secret tunnel inside the oak, and Zoe ran down it, her heart beating fast at the thought of being on Unicorn Island again. The path beneath her feet was soft and warm and she couldn't wait to see the Silvery Glade, with its fluttering, rainbow leaves and azure sky. And most of all, she was longing to see her friend Astra, the little unicorn with the shy smile and sparkling stars on her soft white coat.

This summer had been different than any vacation Zoe had ever had before. She had discovered a magical fairy world, hidden inside the oak tree at the end of her great-aunt's garden, and each adventure had been more enchanting than the last.

But as Zoe rounded the corner, ready to catch her first glimpse of the island, she stopped in shock. Water was lapping over her bare feet. *What's going on?* she wondered. The further she went down the tunnel, the deeper the water became. Soon, it was above her ankles. *It must be coming from the island,* Zoe realized. *But that doesn't make sense. The tunnel has always led straight to the Silvery Glade, and there's no river there...*

Zoe ran the last part of the way, splashing through the water. When she finally emerged from the tunnel she gasped. The Silvery Glade was unrecognizable. There was water everywhere – flooding through the trees and across the grass, leaves swirling on its surface. The clouds hung low and heavy in the sky and even the rainbow leaves seemed to have lost their color. Strangest of all, the glade was completely empty. Usually, Astra would be running through the trees to greet her, while woodland animals darted among the flowers and birds swooped from the branches. But now all was silent, save for the water rushing past.

"Astra?" Zoe called out. "Are you there?"

There was no answer, and even as Zoe stood there, the water was rising. It was swilling around her knees now. She knew she should turn around…follow the trail of light back through the Great Oak, to the safety of her own world. But she couldn't leave Unicorn Island like this. She had to know what was going on and make sure that her friends were safe.

Zoe took a step forward, only to discover the

ground was slipping away from her...and the next moment she was falling into the water. The current was so strong that before she could even cry out, she was swept on, away from the entrance to the Great Oak and through the flooded glade.

The water was icy cold and Zoe looked desperately around for something to hold on to. Ahead of her, she spied a large branch

floating in the water, and she swam frantically towards it. Her fingers grasped the outermost twigs and she pulled them towards her. She edged her way down the branch, but just as she'd wrapped her arms around it, the current gained in strength again.

Faster and faster, Zoe whirled through the Silvery Glade until with a great *WHOOSH!* she shot out from between the trees and into Unicorn Valley.

"Oh no!" Zoe cried. From here, she could see that the waters had spread all across the valley. She couldn't even make out the winding path of the Moon River, or where the flower meadows ended and the gently sloping hills that ringed the valley began. And far above her, in the gray and clouded skies, there was a scattering of unicorns flying hard and fast towards the cliffs. *They must be seeking safety,* she thought, wishing she was up there with them.

"Help!" she called out. "Down here! Help!" But even as she shouted she knew her voice was being drowned out by the rushing water. As far as the eye could see, there was no land, only a vast watery expanse.

Just as she was beginning to lose hope, she

saw a unicorn swooping down towards her from the sky. It wasn't Astra – Zoe would know her anywhere – but as the unicorn came closer she saw with relief that it was Sorrel, Astra's mother, and Guardian of the Trees. She could make out her circlet of ivy, bluebells and passion flowers and the beautiful green

glow to her coat that made it look as if she always carried a part of the forest with her.

"It's okay," Zoe told herself, "I'll be safe now." But then she saw Sorrel's frantic expression, and the way her eyes kept glancing towards something.

Zoe followed her gaze, and her heart began to pound. She'd been so busy looking to the skies that she hadn't seen what lay ahead of her.

The waters had gathered together in a huge swirling whirlpool...and Zoe was being swept straight towards it.

Chapter Two

Zoe gripped on to her branch in fear. She could see now that the whirlpool was sucking everything – flowers, leaves, branches, rocks – towards its foaming center, before dragging them under.

"Sorrel!" Zoe cried. "Quick!"

But as she spoke, the whirlpool caught her in its grip. Zoe began spinning around and around until everything was a blur of gray sky and churning waters. She hugged the branch to her, knowing it was the only thing keeping her afloat.

Then, with a fluttering of gossamer-light wings, Sorrel was at her side. "I'm here," she said, her voice calm and still. "We just need to get you out of the water and on to my back. Reach out with your arm, Zoe, and wrap it around my neck."

"I c-c-can't," Zoe said, through chattering teeth. "I'm too scared. Oh! If only *I* could fly, like you. I'm worried if I let go, I'll be sucked under."

"I won't let that happen," Sorrel replied, her voice still calm, her wings beating steadily above her. "I know you can do this,

Zoe. Just reach out. As soon as you're on my back, I can fly you to safety."

Zoe's mind was telling her to listen to Sorrel, but her fear had somehow locked her arms to the branch and she couldn't bring herself to move them.

"Astra is waiting on the clifftops," Sorrel went on. "I know it's hard, but you need to do this *now*, Zoe."

At Sorrel's words, Zoe glanced towards the whirlpool and saw that she was nearing its center. Any moment now, she would be pulled under. The thought of Astra waiting for her made her feel braver.

Here goes, she decided. And in one swift movement, she flung her arm up to Sorrel's neck. She felt the unicorn lean in towards her, even as her hoofs dipped into the fast-flowing water.

"Now the other arm," said Sorrel. "Quick, Zoe. There's not much time."

With a deep breath, Zoe let go of the branch and reached her other arm around Sorrel's neck. Then she felt Sorrel's wings beating the air as she powered them up and away from the dark center of the whirlpool.

Once they were a little way above the water, Zoe swung her leg over Sorrel's back until she was safely astride her. Then she sank against the warmth of the unicorn's coat.

For a while, Zoe said nothing. Her pajamas clung to her, and her teeth chattered, but all she could feel was relief that she was safe.

As they approached the clifftops, Zoe saw row after row of unicorns, all looking down at the flooded valley in dismay.

"What's happening?" asked Zoe. "What's caused the flood?"

"We think it must be Shadow's work," Sorrel replied. "We've never seen anything like it before. First came the rains. The Cloud Unicorns battled against the storm clouds all night until finally they managed to drive them away. Then, just when we thought we were over the worst, the river began to flood."

Zoe took a sharp intake of breath. "So Shadow's back!" she whispered.

Shadow was an evil fairy pony from an island across the sea, who kept plotting to take over Unicorn Island. Zoe knew he would stop at nothing to get what he wanted – the Unicorn King's crown. If the island was ruined, then the King would have failed in his role to protect it...and Shadow would be free to take over.

"What can we do?" asked Zoe. "Shadow must be stopped!"

"I know," Sorrel replied. "The Guardians have been hard at work trying to protect the unicorns and other animals. The Snow Unicorns are taking everyone to safety in the White Mountains. The Flower Unicorns are trying to protect the birds and butterflies, while I've been busy rescuing the animals of the woods with the other Forest Unicorns. As for the Cloud Unicorns...their spells have stopped the rain from falling,

but the magic they need is so strong, they can't stop chanting or the rains will start again."

Zoe nodded in understanding. She knew that the Guardians were among the most powerful unicorns and that each one protected a different part of Unicorn Island. This time, the situation was so desperate, all the Guardians were helping.

"And what about the King?" she asked.

Sorrel paused for a moment as she scanned the cliff face ahead of them, searching for the best place to land. Zoe held her breath. The King was the most magical of all the unicorns and she desperately hoped he knew a way to stop the floods.

"As soon as the river broke its banks, the King went to the Kingdom of River Unicorns, beneath the waters of Moon River, to ask for help," Sorrel went on. "The River Unicorns control the waters so we think he went to ask them for their most powerful spells. But he hasn't yet come back."

As she spoke, Sorrel stretched out her wings to break her speed and swept down to land on the clifftop. Zoe slid from Sorrel's back and then turned as she heard someone calling her name.

"Astra!" she cried, as she saw the little

unicorn galloping towards her. Zoe could just make out the shining silver stars on her coat and her mother-of-pearl horn, gleaming in the misty air. She wrapped her arms around Astra's neck and breathed in her warm honey scent.

"I'm so glad you're safe," said Astra, in her soft shy voice. "Isn't it terrible, what's happening? At first we thought it was just the rains, but they kept on falling and falling, and then we knew it must be Shadow. When the river burst its banks, there was a great surge of water. So many homes were flooded, so many plants destroyed…"

"It's true," said Sorrel, "and there's so much still to be done to protect everyone. I must go now, to rescue more animals and bring them to higher ground. Zoe and Astra, I want you to stay on the clifftops, where you'll be safe. Take care, both of you."

Zoe nodded. "Thank you, Sorrel," she said.

The unicorn beat her beautiful wings and rose once more into the air. As they watched Sorrel disappear into the clouds, Astra turned to Zoe.

"Oh!" she cried. "You're sopping wet."

"I know," said Zoe, starting to wring out the water from her pajamas. "I suppose that's what happens when you go swimming in whirlpools. So now we wait here?" she added questioningly. But then she saw the gleam in

Astra's eye and smiled. Her friend was never one to stay still. "We're not just going to wait here, are we? What are you planning?"

"We know this is Shadow's work." Astra's voice dropped to a low whisper. "Everyone says the River Unicorns are the only ones who have the power to stop the floods. But the Unicorn King hasn't returned from them with a spell. Something must have gone wrong. I think we should go to the Kingdom of the River Unicorns and investigate."

"What's the Kingdom of the River Unicorns?" Zoe asked uncertainly.

"It's a magical world beneath Moon River," Astra replied. "We just need a little help to get there."

"Oh no you don't!" said a voice.

Zoe and Astra turned to see their friend, Tio, standing close by. His mane was as scruffy as ever, his expression just as serious. He was surrounded by piles of spell books, which Zoe guessed he must have brought with him from the Unicorn King's Castle.

"It's far too dangerous to go to the River Kingdom," Tio said. "The river is swollen by the floods.

You'd be swept away in an instant."

"Just because you're apprentice to the Guardian of the Spells," retorted Astra, "doesn't mean you can tell us what to do."

Tio puffed himself up. "Last time I got caught up in an adventure with you two, I ended up flying around in a storm and nearly fell under a sleep spell. I think I know what I'm talking about."

Zoe could see Astra was about to answer back, so she quickly intervened. "Thank you, Tio," she said, remembering how on her last visit, Tio had helped them stop the storm unleashed by the Box of Winds. "We know that going to the River Kingdom is dangerous, but we can't just stand here and do nothing. Not while the island is suffering like this.

Although…" She looked down as she spoke, at the valley submerged beneath the swirling waters, where only the treetops were visible above the surface. "I'm a little nervous about going back in the water," she admitted. "The current was really strong…"

"Nothing's going to happen to us," said Astra. "Because this time, we'll be protected by magic."

"Whose magic?" asked Tio suspiciously.

"Yours," said Astra. "*You* are going to come with us."

Tio started backing away. "Oh no I'm not. And don't think you can persuade me."

"But, Tio," Astra pleaded, "we *need* you. I don't know the spell to enter the River Kingdom, but I'm sure you do. You're so good at magic. You know *all* the spells."

Tio looked from Zoe to Astra and back again. Both had the same pleading expression.

"If not for us, Tio, then for the island," added Zoe.

"Fine!" humphed Tio. "I'll help you enter the River Kingdom. But that's where my part in this ends."

Zoe and Astra exchanged smiles. "Then we should go right away," said Astra. "Are you ready?"

"Ready," said Zoe. She took a steadying breath, then she swung herself onto Astra's back, tangling her fingers in the unicorn's silky mane.

Tio slipped on his saddlebags, making more huffing noises, and began filling them with his spell books. “It’s important that I take them with me,” he muttered. “You never know when you might need them.”

Then, without another word, Astra and Tio leaped from the cliff face and plunged down across the valley. Zoe held on tight as the wind whistled through her hair.

The misty air hung around them like a cloak as they powered across the island. It was hard to see where the flood waters ended and where Moon River began.

"I think we've reached the center of the valley now," said Astra. "This must be where Moon River runs. The River Kingdom should be just below the surface."

"Yes," added Zoe. "The water seems bluer here. What do we do now?" she asked, suddenly feeling nervous about returning to the water. "Do we just dive in? What happens to us?"

"First I'm going to sprinkle you with magic dust," said Tio. "You cannot enter the River Kingdom without it and it will help protect you." As he spoke, he reached into one of his saddlebags, before blowing a shimmering green dust over them.

At once, Zoe felt a strange tingling sensation spread over her body as the magic began to work. It felt like diving into the sea on a cold day, as if her body were being pricked with goosebumps.

"Now, I'll chant the spell," said Tio. "Say the words with me. As soon as we've finished, the waters should part. That's your moment – you must dive straight into the river. Zoe, you need to be on Astra's back and hold on very tightly."

"I will," promised Zoe.

She tried to quell her fear as she looked down into the churning waters, but as Tio began to chant she barely had time to think. She repeated the lines after him, saying the words in time with Astra...

Waters of the river part,
We come in friendship, true of heart.
Let us safely dive beneath,
We come with promises of peace.

"Good luck!" Tio called, as the surging waters began to part.

"Now!" cried Astra. Zoe gave a final wave, then together, they dived into the river.

Chapter Three

Zoe and Astra dived deeper and deeper beneath the waters. Zoe held her breath, her heart beating wildly. The current pulsed against her and she had to focus on clinging to Astra's back so that she wasn't swept away by the strength of the current, even with the help of the magic dust.

As they swam on, Astra turned to her.

"You can breathe here and talk," she said. "I came with my mother once, a long time ago now. I promise it's safe."

"Are you sure?" Zoe asked, then realized her voice was chiming through the water, as clearly as if she'd spoken on land.

Astra nodded. "Your clothes will stay dry too – the sparkling dust protects you. The River Unicorns are shy and like to keep themselves to themselves, which is why the other unicorns don't visit too often."

Now that Zoe's first shock of entering the

water was over, she could begin to look around. She saw beautiful houses, woven from rushes and reeds, being torn apart by the current. Brightly colored fish darted between the river plants, desperately seeking shelter, and every now and then other creatures would rush past them – turtles, dolphins, otters – but there was no sign of the River Unicorns.

"Here," said Astra. "There's a rock we can shelter behind. The current won't buffet us so much here."

"How are we going to find the River Unicorns?" Zoe asked, relieved she could rest for a moment. "Do you know where they live?"

"You don't have to worry," Astra replied. "They'll find us. They have a way of knowing what's going on in their kingdom. But I hope they come quickly. The river current is so strong. It's hard just to keep swimming forwards."

Just then, a group of unicorns appeared out of the watery shadows. Their coats seemed to reflect the colors of the river, dappled blue and green, and Zoe noticed their wings shimmered and dazzled like dragonflies'.

"Greetings," said the first River Unicorn to reach them. "I am Iris, the new apprentice to the Guardian of the River."

"Greetings," Astra replied. "We've come about the floods."

Iris nodded – rather haughtily, Zoe thought. "We noticed the rains first," Iris said. "That's when the river first began to swell. But then came a terrifying torrent of water and it felt as if some dreadful magic was forcing all the sea inland. We're doing everything we can to send the water back to the sea, but the spell we need is in the Grimoire – the very book stolen by Shadow."

Zoe gazed at Astra. "Does that mean the River Unicorns don't have the spell we need?" she asked in an undertone. "What about the King? Where has he gone?"

"I have seen him," said another voice.

Zoe looked up and saw a beautiful River Unicorn, with sparkling dragonfly wings and a circlet of water lilies upon her head.

"I am Naida, Guardian of the River Unicorns," she said. "All is not lost. There is another copy of the spell that controls the waters of the sea and which will stop these floods. Legend says it's kept in a deserted underwater palace, where the river meets the sea. The Unicorn King has gone there – to see if he can find the spell."

The other River Unicorns gasped and began muttering between themselves in anxious voices.

"What is it?" Zoe asked. "What's wrong?"

"I've heard of the deserted palace," Astra replied, her gaze fixed on Naida. "An evil unicorn named Damerel lived there, a long time ago. It is said that when he died, he cursed the palace. No one knows what the curse is, or what could trigger it, so no one dares enter the palace to find its secret spells or hidden treasures."

"All you say is true, Astra," replied Naida. "No one has ever entered the palace for fear of the curse. But the King had no choice. That spell is our only hope. And for all we know, the legend may not be true."

"Then why did the King go alone?" asked Astra, quietly.

Naida looked at Astra closely. "Your questions are deep, for such a young unicorn," she replied. "The King went on his own as he knew the mission could be dangerous. He didn't want to risk a life other than his own."

"Shouldn't he be back by now?" asked Zoe.

Naida sighed. "I have begun to worry," she admitted. "But I can't go looking for him – my duty is here. We are doing all we can to hold back the surging waters. I know that the river is flooding, but without our spells, it would be even worse than it is now."

"We can go," said Zoe urgently. "If the legend is true, then the King may be in need of our help."

"His life could be in danger," added Astra.

But Naida shook her head. "Zoe does not have our powers, and I know your magic isn't always with you, Astra. I could never forgive myself if something happened. And the current will only get stronger as you head towards the sea."

Astra hung her head and Zoe saw the sorrow in her eyes. Unlike all the other unicorns on the island, Astra wasn't always able to do magic. But Zoe couldn't bear to see her this sad.

"It's true that Astra can't always do magic," she told Naida. "But it's always come when she needs it most, and when I'm with her. And then her magic is even stronger than the other unicorns'. We've fought off danger before. I know we can do it again."

At this, Astra raised her head, smiling gratefully at Zoe. "And the longer we leave the King, the more damage the floods will do to Unicorn Island. We don't have much time to stop Shadow."

Naida looked at the other River Unicorns, who nodded in agreement.

"It's true," said one. "The King should have returned by now. And even down here we have heard tales of these visitors – the unicorn with stars on her back and the human child. They have fought against Shadow's spells before."

There was a moment's pause. "You may go then," Naida said, with a sigh. "But I cannot send you alone. Iris," she called. "Please go with Astra and Zoe. Show them the way to the Underwater Palace and then bring them safely back again. Whatever you do, keep together. When you reach the palace, call for the King, but do not go in yourselves."

Iris swam to the front. Her glistening green coat sparkled in the water, but it seemed to Zoe as if she was almost swelling with a sense of her own importance.

"Iris is one of my most capable and sensible unicorns," said Naida. "You'll be safe with her."

Zoe tried smiling at her, but Iris simply

nodded in return.

"You need to head downriver, towards the sea," Naida went on. "The entrance to the palace has long been hidden under a curtain of seaweed, but you can find it by following a trail of golden shells on the river floor. I know I can trust in your bravery. Good luck, and stay safe."

Chapter Four

As soon as Naida had spoken, and without a word to the others, Iris began swimming downriver, her wings beating fast as she moved swiftly through the water. Zoe and Astra followed as quickly as they could, though Zoe could feel the force of the current against them, pushing its way up from the sea.

"Thank you for taking us," said Astra.

But Iris only turned to them and sniffed. "I actually have better things to do than chaperone you two down the river," she said. "I don't believe a word of this so-called legend. I don't know why you've taken it upon yourselves to try and save the King when I'm sure he doesn't need saving."

"Oh," said Zoe, stung by her words.

"So...you don't believe in the curse at all?" Astra added.

"Of course not," Iris replied. "Unicorns love telling stories – it doesn't mean they're true. Some River Unicorns say the palace is haunted by a terrible ghost, others that a monster lives there. I never listen to that type of thing. And I don't want to hear one more word about it from you two," she added disapprovingly.

Zoe didn't know what to make of Iris's words. Was the curse just a fairy tale? Or was there truth behind the stories?

"What's more," added Iris, "I've heard the River Unicorns talking about you two down here. I expect you think you're very important, saving the island from Shadow –"

"No, not at all," Astra began to say.

But Iris continued as if she hadn't spoken. "– but there's no need for you both to get big-headed about it."

"We're not!" protested Zoe, but Iris had turned her head again and was obviously ignoring them.

"She's not very friendly, is she?" Astra whispered to Zoe, as soon as Iris was out of earshot. Zoe could see she looked hurt.

"No," admitted Zoe. "She's probably heard about everything you've done and feels jealous. I'm sure that's all it is."

Astra still looked upset.

"What else do you know about the curse?" she asked Astra. Zoe wanted to distract her, but she was also eager to find out more.

"I don't know much more," Astra replied, keeping her voice low. "I know it's said that Damerel longed to rule over Unicorn Island, just like Shadow. He wanted his Underwater Palace to be fit for a king and stole all the treasures he could find so that it would be grander than anything else on the island. But when the Unicorn King found out what he was doing, he banished Damarel to his palace, and Damarel was never allowed to leave."

"What kind of treasures?" asked Zoe.

"Oh!" said Astra. "Jewels, beautiful statues and powerful spells. The most precious of all is supposed to be the Black Pearl, which grants a single wish to whoever opens its shell first."

"And do you think the story about the curse is true?" asked Zoe.

Astra glanced ahead at Iris to make sure she wasn't listening. "Naida seemed to believe it," she said. "And the Unicorn King must have thought it might be true, or he wouldn't have gone to the palace on his own, to avoid anyone else getting hurt..."

Zoe nodded solemnly.

"Do you want to turn back?" asked Astra.

"Of course not," said Zoe. "We have to stop the floods. I'll do whatever I can."

After that, they swam on in silence. As the current grew stronger, Zoe found that even seeing what lay ahead became difficult. The water was full of flotsam from the sea – pieces of seaweed, sand and pebbles. Sea grasses tangled in her hair and every now and then fronds of seaweed covered her eyes.

"I'm not sure how much longer I can keep swimming," Astra called out. "The current is so strong here."

"It's not far now," said Iris. "Keep close behind me. The entrance should be just around this corner."

"Oh look!" cried Zoe excitedly. Through the murky water, she could just make out a line of golden shells making a trail along the riverbed. Cautiously, Zoe swam forwards. She gave a little gasp. Ahead of her was a curtain of seaweed, just as Naida had described. As it waved in the current, Zoe glimpsed a door behind it, covered in yet more golden shells. "The Underwater Palace!" she said. "We've found it!"

"Yes, I knew it was here," said Iris. Zoe thought the River Unicorn sounded sulky that she hadn't been the first to spot it. "Get behind me, please," she added bossily.

But at that moment, there was a great roaring sound. The waters around the entrance of the cave began to swirl and thicken and, when Zoe looked again, a huge, dark shape was coming towards them, as if emerging from the cloud of water.

"What is it?" Zoe cried.

"I don't know," said Astra. "But get back, Zoe!"

Iris rushed over to Astra and Zoe, watching in horror as the dark shape began to circle them, taking form before their eyes. It had a long, snakelike body, black as night, with bright, unblinking eyes. Its tail whipped through the water.

"It's a m-m-monster!" gasped Iris. "The legend is true! If I'd known, I never would have come." The River Unicorn's body began to quiver with fear. "And look!" she added. "What are those sharp pointy things? I think

it's got teeth. We have to get out of here."

"But what about the Unicorn King?" asked Astra.

"I'm sure he has the power to fight off a monster," said Iris. "But I don't know if I do. Naida should never have sent us here. I have to go back."

The snakelike creature was drawing ever-closer circles around them. Zoe could have reached out and touched its slimy scales. It fixed its eyes on them, seeming to trap them in its mesmerizing gaze...

"Can you say a spell, Iris?" asked Zoe. "Something to ward it off?"

But Iris was so gripped by fear, she couldn't

answer. Zoe turned to Astra.

"I'm *trying* to think of something," said Astra. "But I've never met a monster before. I'm not sure I know how to fight one."

"Well, think fast," said Zoe. "Because that creature is getting closer. And by the look of those teeth, I don't think we can fight it off without magic."

Iris let out a low moan while Astra frowned, concentrating hard. "Okay," Astra said, after a deep breath. "I've got one, but I have no idea if it will work."

Zoe looked over at the entrance to the palace. "Astra," she said, "this could be our only chance to rescue the King. Why don't I swim as fast as I can towards the entrance of the palace? That'll distract the creature and give you a chance to say the spell."

"Are you crazy?" said Iris.

"You can't go into the palace," added Astra. "What about the hidden curse? What happens if you trigger it?"

"I've been thinking about that," Zoe went on. "Everyone says it's a curse for unicorns. Maybe, being a human, I'll be safe..."

Astra looked grim. "It's a very risky plan," she said.

"It's not risky, it's insane," said Iris.

Zoe pointed at the terrifying creature. Its staring eyes were still fixed on them and it had started making a low hissing noise, its forked tongue flicking out into the water.

"Astra, it looks like it's going to attack us. We don't have a choice," she went on. "The palace entrance is just over there. If I distract it we've got a chance of defeating it. Once I've gone in, and you've fought off the monster, you and Iris can head back for help."

Zoe turned to Iris, to see if she was going to object again, but the River Unicorn had closed her eyes, as if to block the monster out.

"Fine," said Astra. "I'll start chanting the spell. Get ready to swim..."

Zoe waited tensely, as Astra began to speak the words of the spell:

Creature of the waters deep,
Return now to your quiet sleep...

Without stopping to hear the rest of the spell, Zoe made a dash for the palace. It was only a short distance away, but the current was at its strongest here and she had to swim as hard as she could. To her horror, she could hear the swish of the monster's body behind her, the thrashing of its tail as it powered through the water.

As soon as she reached the curtain of seaweed she swept it back and looked desperately for a latch to the door. But the door was covered in a thick green cloak of sea slime. Her heart pounding, Zoe ran her hands over the slippery surface. To her surprise, it swung open at her touch with a loud creaking noise. Zoe braved a final glance over her shoulder, just in time to see the sea monster racing towards her, its mouth agape, gnashing its dagger-sharp teeth. Zoe didn't wait a moment longer. She swam inside and slammed the door shut behind her.

Panting hard, Zoe began to make her way down the corridor before her. It was carved into the rock and she had no choice but to swim down it. *Don't think about the curse,* she told herself. *Or what might be happening to Astra. I'm sure her spell will work. What I have to do now is find the King...*

Before long, the corridor opened out into a wide, square courtyard with a smooth marble floor. It was surrounded by golden walls, and statues of unicorns, gleaming with mother-of-pearl, stood in each corner. Fish darted in and

out, while reeds snaked up through cracks in the floor. Even though it was beautiful, Zoe couldn't help but shiver. There was something eerie about the Underwater Palace.

Looking up, she saw row upon row of empty windows and even though she was desperate to find the Unicorn King, she felt too afraid to call out. She chose a passage at random and quickly made her way down it, looking left and right into the large, empty rooms. *Somewhere here,* she thought, *there must be the treasure chest with the spell to call the waters back to the sea.*

Hopefully, when she found it, she'd find the Unicorn King, too.

As she made her way around the palace, Zoe couldn't shake off the feeling that someone was following her. Every corner she turned, she heard a clatter of hoof beats and once, out of the corner of her eye, she was sure that she saw a white shape flitting behind a doorway. *What could it be?* she wondered. *Is this the ghost that Iris spoke of?*

Zoe began to move faster now, desperate to find the King. But at the same time, the frantic hoof beats grew louder and doors banged and creaked around her. She took off down another corridor, glancing over her shoulder. Then, to Zoe's horror, she collided with something hard and warm…and screamed.

Chapter Five

Zoe froze in fear. She couldn't bear to see what she'd crashed into. But she knew she had to find out. She whipped her head around...

"Astra!" she cried.

There was her friend, ghostly white in the dark waters of the palace, looking just as surprised to see her. Zoe flung her arms around Astra's neck and hugged her tight.

"I was desperately trying to find the spell and the King and then I thought someone was following me and I started going faster and faster..."

"I could hear you moving," Astra replied, "but I was convinced it was the ghost, or something to do with the curse... I was running away from you too!"

They looked at each other and laughed for a moment, too relieved to do anything else.

"What happened with the monster?" Zoe asked. "And where's Iris? I thought you were going back with her."

"The spell seemed to work," Astra said. "But I don't think it was a real monster at all. After I had chanted the words, it disappeared in a swirl of darkness, as if it was no more than an illusion. Then Iris insisted we go back to the other River Unicorns, but I couldn't bring myself to leave you here, so I entered the palace."

"But what about the curse?" said Zoe.

Astra shrugged. "Maybe it isn't true. I haven't felt anything yet. But even if it is, our first priority is to find the King."

Zoe nodded. "Do you have any idea where he might be? This palace is like a maze. It seems to go on and on forever."

Astra shook her head. "I've looked around all the rooms and corridors down here and

I've been upstairs, too..." She looked thoughtful for a moment. "Hang on," she said suddenly. "When I was outside in the courtyard I saw a turret. Did you see it too? That's the only place I haven't checked. Could that be where the treasure chest is kept?"

Zoe smiled at her. "Well remembered," she said. "Astra, you're always so great at working things out."

"Hoofs crossed..." Astra replied. "Follow me. I think the stairs to the turret are this way."

As Zoe set off behind Astra along yet more twisting corridors, she couldn't help a little shiver. Glinting jewels studded the walls and everywhere she looked there were more statues, all of the same unicorn, with a crown on his head, smiling cruelly. Zoe guessed they must be of Damerel.

"I feel like we're being watched," Zoe said to Astra. "There's something evil about this place."

"I feel the same," said Astra. "Maybe it's Damerel's wicked magic at work. Or maybe it's part of the palace's curse. It's like the walls are trying to push us away. But we don't have any choice. We have to keep going."

At last they came to a thin set of spiraling steps that wound their way up a narrow tower.

Astra swam up them, with Zoe following close behind. Finally, the steps came to an abrupt stop in front of a closed wooden door set in a pointed archway.

"What if this room holds the curse?" asked Zoe.

"We've come too far now – we've got to find the King and the spell, whatever it takes," said Astra.

Zoe nodded, and together they pushed at the door. It fell open easily, as if inviting them in.

Zoe's first thought was that she'd entered a fairy tale. The room was bathed in a clear light and she found herself transfixed by a treasure chest in the corner, which sparkled with magic dust. It seemed to be lit by an inner glow. Mesmerized, Zoe and Astra walked towards it.

"Stop!" cried a voice suddenly, weak but determined.

Zoe and Astra broke out of their trance and gasped in dismay. There was the Unicorn King, lying in a heap next to the chest.

The last time Zoe had seen the King, he had towered above her, his majestic crown glinting in the sunlight, the blue-black sheen of his coat glowing with health. Now he appeared shrunken and weak, his body stretched out across the floor, his beautiful butterfly wings folded against his sides.

"What's happened?" cried Astra, rushing over to him. "Who has done this to you?"

"The curse..." whispered the King, his voice hoarse. "Whatever you do, don't open the treasure chest. That's where the curse lies.

The palace itself has been steeped in magic, but only to make any unicorn feel unsettled, so they wish to get away. But Damerel put the full force of his evil into protecting the chest, as that is where the real treasure lies. Any unicorn who opens it has all their power and strength sucked from them."

"What can we do?" asked Zoe. "How can we help?"

"Here," said the King, and he passed Zoe a piece of parchment, scrawled with the words of a spell. "This is the spell to reverse the floodwaters and save Unicorn Island. I want you both to swim upriver, back the way you came. You'll need the

River Unicorns and the Guardians to make the spell work. And I need you to hurry. We don't have much time. As soon as the waters reach my castle, there will be no reversing the spell and Shadow will have won – he will be free to take over the island."

Zoe clutched the parchment tight. "But we can't just leave you here," said Astra, tears in her eyes.

"You must," replied the King. "I'm too weak to make the journey, and if you stay to help me, there'll be no time to save the island from the waters."

"This was all part of Shadow's plan, wasn't it?" said Zoe. "He must have known you'd try and find the spell, and that you'd be cursed."

"Yes," the King replied. "But I had no choice. Unicorn Island needs that spell, and I couldn't have asked another unicorn to get it for me. And there is a chance I can get my strength back. But first, you *must* cast that spell. Don't fail me."

"We won't," Astra promised.

They turned to go, even though it broke Zoe's heart to leave him there, lying on the floor like a newborn foal.

"There's nothing we can do for him now except help save the island," said Astra, as they raced back through the palace. "Climb on my back, Zoe, and we'll swim together."

As they neared the entrance to the palace, Astra bent her head determinedly, her wings beating furiously as she drove them forwards, back up the river.

This time, they weren't fighting against the current. Instead it pushed them quickly back towards the River Unicorns. As they reached the spot where they'd first entered the river, Zoe could see the River Unicorns waiting for them with anxious expressions on their faces. Iris was among them, though she looked less haughty now.

"We were just coming to find you," said Naida, coming forwards to greet them. "Iris told us that you'd gone into the palace."

"I tried to stop them!" Iris insisted. "But then the monster came and..." She stopped and shuddered.

"We did go into the palace," said Astra in a rush. "We found the Unicorn King and we have the spell. But it's just as we feared – he's been cursed."

"Then I must go to him," said Naida.

Zoe shook her head. "He made us promise that first you would help cast the spell to save Unicorn Island. As soon as the waters enter the King's Castle, it will be too late. The spell cannot be reversed."

"Then we must hurry," said another River Unicorn. "We've just looked above the surface to check on the floods and to let the other Guardians know what was happening. The water is lapping at the castle steps as we speak."

Chapter Six

Zoe glanced around the other unicorns, seeing the panic on their faces. No one could bear the thought of what would happen if Shadow took over the island. Only Naida looked calm. "Then let us head to the surface at once," she said. "From there, I'll summon the other Guardians."

On beating dragonfly wings, the River Unicorns rose to the surface, emerging from the water in a dazzling throng, their bodies glistening with spray. Zoe was shocked to see that the floodwaters had risen even further. Waves were now beginning to lap at the door of the Unicorn King's Castle.

"To the cliff face," commanded Naida. "We'll summon the other Guardians from there."

As one, they took off for dry land, their hoofs skimming the churning waters. As soon as they landed, Naida blew long and hard on a conch shell. Its call echoed across the gray skies.

At last, to her relief, Zoe saw the Guardians fly to the clifftops to join them. Eira, Guardian of the Snow, swooped down from the White Mountains, Nimbus came down from the clouds. From across the waters came Sorrel, her coat gleaming green like the forest, and Lily, Guardian of the Flowers, soared in from the west on outspread wings.

"Thank you for coming," said Naida, as they touched down beside her. "We have the spell to send the waters back to the sea. It has come from the King himself but he cannot join us

now. We must say it together and I know it will take all our strength."

"We're ready," said Sorrel solemnly.

Naida nodded and looked at Zoe. "Please," she said, "hold up the spell."

Zoe unfolded the piece of parchment and held it up for all the Guardians and River Unicorns to see.

"We'll say it together," said Naida, "and then each of us must fly over a different part of the island, to drive the waters back. If you head back the way you came, then we should achieve our mission. Astra," she added, "I'd like you to say the spell with us."

Astra nodded, and Zoe could see the anxiety in her eyes, that she might let the Guardians down.

"Then let us begin," said Naida.

As one, the Guardians began to chant:

The voices of the unicorns rose together and flooded across the sky, seeming to sweep over the surface of the waters. But even though they chanted the words again and again, nothing seemed to happen. Zoe looked over at Astra and she knew that her magic hadn't come. The stars on her coat were dull, her eyes anxious.

"My magic..." Astra whispered, and Zoe could see tears sliding down her face. "It's not coming. It worked before against the monster...but maybe I've used it all up? I wish I was like the other unicorns. Why can't I do magic like them?"

Zoe came over to her. "Let me climb on your back," she said. "I'll say the words too. I'm sure the magic will work if we try it together."

Numbly, Astra nodded and bent her legs so that Zoe could climb on her back. Then Zoe began to chant the words with her, closing her eyes and pouring all her concentration into imagining the waters seeping back to the sea.

"Oh!" cried Astra. "I can feel something – I think it's the magic. It's tingling in my hoofs and in my horn."

Zoe opened her eyes and smiled wide. "It is!" she said. "The stars on your coat are glowing. That's always a sign. And look!" she added, pointing to the floodwaters. She watched, mesmerized, as the waves seemed to respond to the words of the spell, rising up and folding back on themselves, until they began to flow back towards the sea.

"Astra, Zoe," Naida called, "I can feel the strength of your magic. Follow the course of the river and drive its waters back into the sea."

Astra took to the skies and together she and Zoe chanted the words of the spell, over and

over. To Zoe's joy, she saw that the floodwaters were starting to recede. Sparkles were shooting out from Astra's horn as she chanted, and it seemed as if the sparkles called to the water, pushing it back into the sea.

"We're winning," said Zoe.

They flew on towards the sea, driving a wall of water ahead of them. As it crashed into the sea, Zoe turned and a smile lit her face.

"I think we're done," she whispered to Astra. Slowly but surely, Unicorn Island was emerging from the flood. The remaining water was returning to the river. First the tops of trees showed through in the Silvery Glade, then the banks of Moon River came into view

once more, until, finally, the green stems of the grasses poked up above the waterline.

A great cheer came from the clifftops as the other unicorns realized that the danger had finally passed. Above them, yet more unicorns began to stream down from the sky, returning from the safety of the White Mountains.

"I think we've done it!" cried Zoe, hardly daring to believe it. "We've beaten Shadow!"

"We have," said Astra, grinning back at her as she came to land on the riverbank.

"It's all thanks to you two, for finding the spell," said Sorrell, coming over to greet them.

"But what about the King?" asked Astra.

"We'll go back for him now," said Naida. "I'll go myself—"

"Wait!" cried Zoe. "What's that?"

She pointed down to the river water, which had begun to bubble and froth at the surface. The next moment the waters parted and the Unicorn King shot up into the sky, his shimmering wings beating fast. He gazed around the island, a smile on his face, then fluttered down to the riverbank.

"You saved the island," he said to the Guardians, his voice almost a whisper. "That's all I needed to know."

And with those words, he sank to the ground, unmoving.

Chapter Seven

The Guardians rushed over to where the King lay, and Zoe could hear them chanting spells beneath their breath. But try as they might, the King stayed still, his wings flat against his back, his body weak and crumpled.

"It was when he opened the treasure chest," Astra explained. "That's when the curse struck. He said it sapped his strength and power."

Naida's face looked grim. "If it's Damerel's curse then we cannot reverse the spell without the Grimoire."

"Our best hope now is to return to the castle and read the spell books," said Sorrell. "There must be something we can do."

"Look!" cried Zoe. "I think he's moving."

The King was tugging open the bag around his neck. A moment later, out fell an oyster shell, gleaming with a light of its own.

As if the effort had used up the last of his strength, the King lowered his head once more and closed his eyes.

"What is it?" Zoe asked.

Naida gave a faint smile. "Our King has

thought of everything," she said. "It's the Black Pearl. Legend said it, too, was in the treasure chest."

Medwen, Guardian of the Spells, made his way through the crowd, closely followed by Tio. Medwen gazed at the shell solemnly.

"The Black Pearl has the power to grant your deepest desire. All you have to do is open the shell. As soon as you see its magical glow, you can make your wish."

"Does that mean we can open it and wish

for the King to be well again?" asked Zoe.

Naida shook her head. "It's not as simple as that," she said. "The Black Pearl isn't really a force for good. It exerts a pull on whoever opens it to wish for whatever *they* most want. It dredges up your deepest, most selfish desires. I'd be too afraid to open it. And it can be used only once. If only the King had the strength to open it for himself..."

Zoe looked over to the other Guardians, who had all taken a step back. "I don't know if I dare open it either," said Sorrell. "Its pull is said to be extremely strong. What if I held it and I wished instead for the safety of my trees? Or something for Astra?"

"Let's discuss this together," said Naida.

The Guardians huddled in a group. Zoe

turned her eyes to the King, and wished the Guardians would hurry. His breathing was getting shallower, and it was almost as if he was shrinking before her eyes.

"Astra?" asked Zoe. "Can't you open it?"

But even Astra shook her head. "What if I wished for my magic to be with me always?" she said. "I wish I could trust myself, but I'm not sure I can."

At last, Naida lifted her head. "We've made our decision," she said. "Zoe, we'd like you to open the Black Pearl, and wish for the King's recovery. As unicorns, we fear we won't be able to overcome its powers and that we'll wish for something for ourselves. As a human, with no other ties in our world, we hope you'll have the strength to think only of the King."

Zoe froze for a moment, thoughts tumbling through her mind. What if she wished for something else? Something for herself? But she knew there wasn't time. She had to do what the Guardians asked...and she had to hope she did it right.

Astra nodded at her encouragingly and Zoe bent down to pick up the oyster shell. She stood, her fingers tracing its rough and jagged edges. It looked like any ordinary shell but she could feel the magic pulsing within it. The shell seemed to tingle and quiver in her hands, like a living thing, inviting her to open it. With a last look at the King, Zoe slowly pried it apart. At once, its powerful magic began coursing through her veins. Her gaze was fixed on the single black pearl, lying in the center of the shell, shining with a strange, unearthly light.

At once, a million different desires rushed through her mind – she saw herself with wings, able to fly like the unicorns. Then she saw herself full of powerful magic, able to defeat Shadow single-handedly. As the thoughts raced through her head, another wish came to her, one she didn't even know she had – to be able to stay on Unicorn Island forever.

Then she heard a quiet voice in her ear. "Zoe," said Astra. "The King. Think of the King."

Zoe forced herself to look over at him again, and to think what would happen if he never recovered. *I wish for the King to get better*, she chanted to herself. *I wish for the King to get better*. Saying the words inside her head, she held the shell in front of the King.

At once, a dazzling glow spilled out from the center of the pearl, bathing the King in its light.

As the unicorns gathered around, the King began to stir – slowly, but surely. First his eyes opened, then he stood up on shaking legs, opened his mouth and whinnied long and loud.

"Thank you, Zoe," he said, his voice deep and rumbling once more. "You have saved me."

The King took a step forward and stumbled, once, twice, then began to walk forward. "My strength is returning," he muttered to himself. "I can feel it. Yes, it's coming." With a neigh and a great toss of his head he broke into a canter, then a gallop until at last he began to beat his wings so he was flying high above the river. And as he soared above the island, Zoe saw golden dust raining down. To her astonishment, she realized this was more magic. Each speck of golden dust was like a ray of sun, drying out the land.

"Look!" cried Astra. "The animals are returning."

As the Unicorn King swooped back over the Flower Meadows, Zoe could see squirrels, rabbits and hedgehogs making their way

down from the hillside, running back to their forest homes, and the sky was filled with birdsong once more.

The Unicorn King looked down at the Guardians, his face bearing a rare smile.

"You made the right choice asking Zoe to open the shell," he said. "Only she could have wished for my safety. The selfish pull of the Black Pearl is too strong for a unicorn to fight. That is why I have never used it. No unicorn can trust itself with its power."

The King gazed across the island. "Once again," he continued, "we have defeated Shadow. The danger has passed and our island is restored to us."

At this, a great cheer went up from the unicorns, and then Naida fluttered over until she was hovering beside the King.

"To celebrate the end of the flood and the safe return of our King, you are all invited to the River Kingdom for a dance!" she said.

At this, an even louder cheer went up. Astra and Zoe looked at each other and grinned.

"Follow me," said Naida. And one by one, the unicorns chanted the spell to enter the River Kingdom and dived after her into the crystal-clear waters. Zoe leaped onto Astra's back and this time, as they entered the water, she could really take in the beauty of this underwater world. All around her, the other unicorns sped by in flashes of color, fish darting between them, and the waters were filled with the sound of music as the River Unicorns picked up their instruments. They played on reed harps and conch shells, on ribbon-tied bells and spiraling seashell flutes.

Astra and Zoe hung back a moment just to watch, as the unicorns swayed in time to the music, weaving and circling, tossing their

heads and swishing their tails. Then Astra smiled at Zoe "Let's dance!" she said.

Zoe thought nothing could be as magical as joining in the underwater dance. She slid from Astra's back and swam with the others as they swirled through the warm, silky water.

Through the reeds, she noticed Iris swimming towards them.

"Astra, Zoe," she said. "I'm so sorry about the way I treated you. I was jealous of all you had done…and then when that monster appeared, I was too scared to fight him. I feel as if I've failed."

Astra shook her head. "You did everything Naida asked of you," she said. "And we didn't leave you with much choice. Zoe and I completely disobeyed Naida's orders."

"Well, I'm glad you did," said Iris, smiling now. "But I can see I still have a lot to learn."

With those words, she swam away to join the other River Unicorns, looking much less proud and haughty now.

As darkness gathered in the skies above the

river and the waters were lit by the shining stones of the riverbed, Sorrel beckoned to Zoe and Astra, and they left the dance to join her.

"Zoe, I know you want to stay," she said, "but night is drawing in and it is time for you to return to your world, so you can get some sleep before morning comes. Astra, will you fly Zoe to the entrance to the Great Oak?"

"Of course," said Astra, smiling.

"And, Zoe," Sorrel went on, "like the King, I want to thank you for everything you did today. Without you, we may not have been able to save the King – or the island. Now goodbye, and fly well."

Zoe slipped her arms around Astra's neck and waved goodbye to Sorrel. They began to head for the surface and broke through in a shower of starlit spray.

As they winged their way back across Unicorn Island, they were both silent for a while, lost in thought. Astra spoke first.

"Together," she said, "we can do powerful magic, Zoe. Wasn't it amazing, watching the floodwaters being driven back into the sea?"

"It was," Zoe agreed. "And I'm sure your magic is getting stronger all the time."

"I hope so," said Astra, smiling. "With you on my back, I know I have the power to do great magic. For now, that's enough for me."

"Oh!" said Zoe, hugging Astra tight. "I'm so glad that I can help."

All too soon, they reached the entrance to the Great Oak. Zoe slid from Astra's back and gave her one last hug.

"Promise you'll come again soon?" said Astra.

"I promise," said Zoe.

And with that, she ran down the tunnel through the Great Oak, back to her own world. This time, more than any other, she couldn't help her face being wreathed in smiles. She had saved the Unicorn King. She had really helped. And she couldn't wait for more adventures on Unicorn Island.

Edited by Becky Walker

Designed by Brenda Cole

Reading consultant: Alison Kelly

First published in 2017 by Usborne Publishing Ltd.,
Usborne House, 83-85 Saffron Hill, London EC1N 8RT, England.
www.usborne.com

This edition first published in America in 2018

Front cover and inside illustrations by Nuno Vieira Alexandre

A CIP catalogue record for this book is available from the British Library.